This edition published by Parragon Books Ltd in 2015 and distributed by

Parragon Inc.
440 Park Avenue South, 13th Floor
New York, NY 10016
www.parragon.com

ISBN 978-1-4748-0146-1

Printed in China

Disney
FROZEN

ANNA AND ELSA'S
BOOK OF SECRETS

PaRragon

Bath • New York • Cologne • Melbourne • Delhi
Hong Kong • Shenzhen • Singapore • Amsterdam

This book
belongs to

What Makes You, You?

After a long time living separate lives, Anna and Elsa had to get to know each other all over again. Now they want to get to know you, too!

My name is ....

If I could have any name I wanted, it would be

....

My birthday is

Circle the month and day.

Jan	May	Sept
Feb	June	Oct
Mar	July	Nov
Apr	Aug	Dec

1	2	3	4	5
6	7	8	9	10
11	12	13	14	15
16	17	18	19	20
21	22	23	24	25
26	27	28	29	
30	31			

I'm really good at ....

....

....

If I had a superpower, it would be

....

....

It always makes me laugh when

....

....

Something I have in common
with ELSA is

....

....

Something I have in common
with ANNA is

....

....

Three words that best
describe me are

1 ....

2 ....

3 ....

Two words my friends and family would use to describe me are

1 ....   2 ....

Your Family Story

Family is very important to Anna and Elsa. When Elsa turned 21, she followed her family destiny to become Queen of Arendelle. What's unique and special about your family?

Who's in your family?
Write the names of your family
members in the boxes below.

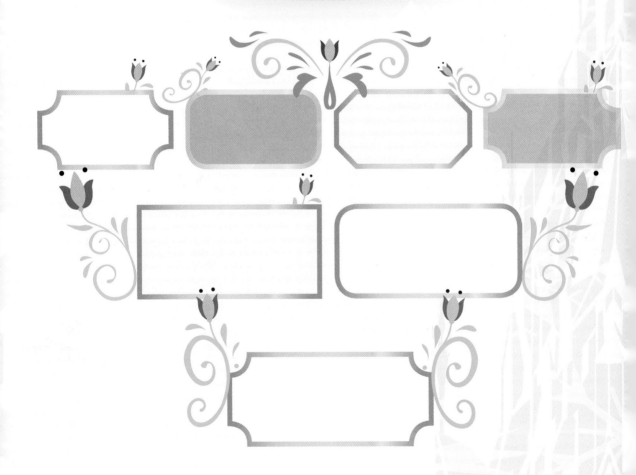

I was born in a place called ....

....

My family is special because ....

....

....

....

My three favorite
things to do with
my family are

1 ....

2 ....

3 ....

Making Memories

Anna and Elsa like to keep lots of photos around their home to remind them of their parents. Use these pages to make a special collection of your favorite family photos.

Who's who in each photo? Write their names underneath.

Sharing Secrets

Elsa used to keep a big secret from Anna, but now these sisters share everything! Do you have someone special you like to share your secrets with? Write about them below. Don't worry, your secrets are safe with Anna and Elsa!

I share my secrets with ....

....

I trust them with my secrets because ....

....

They trust me with their secrets because ....

....

The biggest secret I've shared with them is ....

....

The biggest secret they've shared with me is ....

....

Paste a picture
of you and your
friend here.

Friends Forever

When Anna saved Elsa's life, they both realized that their love for each other could overcome anything. Can you think of a time you've done something special for a friend in need? Write about it below.

Something special I have done for a friend

....

....

....

Something special a friend has done for me

....

....

....

Anna and Elsa know your friends are important to you, just like they are important to each other! Fill in these details about your best friends.

My friend's name is ....

We have known each other for ....

Our favorite thing to do together is ....

....

My friend makes me happy because ....

....

My friend's name is ....

We have known each other for ....

Our favorite thing to do together is ....

....

My friend makes me happy because ....

....

Friendship Album

Anna and Elsa treasure every moment with each other and their friends. Do you have lots of cute photographs of funny moments, special occasions, and epic adventures with your friends? Paste them in here!

Who's who in each photo? Write their names underneath.

Traveling Together

Anna and Elsa love going on adventures—especially together! Do you have an adventure partner you like to share your experiences with? Tell Anna and Elsa all about them below.

My adventure partner is ....

We like to go on adventures to ....

....

Our favorite adventure together was ....

....

....

My favorite thing about my adventure partner is ....

....

....

Our next adventure will be to ....

....

....

Draw or paste in a picture of the place you and your adventure partner would like to go next!

Do You Want to Build a Snowman?

When she was little, Elsa built a snowman called Olaf for Anna. Olaf walks and talks and he loves warm hugs! Now it's your turn to create your very own snowman friend!

I would like to build my snowman with ....

My snowman's name is ....

My snowman's favorite thing is ....

My snowman's favorite season is:

Summer ☐   Winter ☐

Fall ☐   Spring ☐

My snowman dreams of ....

The best thing about my snowman is ....

....

Draw your
very own
snowman here!

Fears and Worries

Elsa used to worry about people discovering her icy powers, until Anna helped her to overcome her fears. Do you have a secret fear or worry like Elsa's? Write about it below.

My secret fear is ....

....

It makes me feel worried because ....

....

When I feel worried, it helps to ....

....

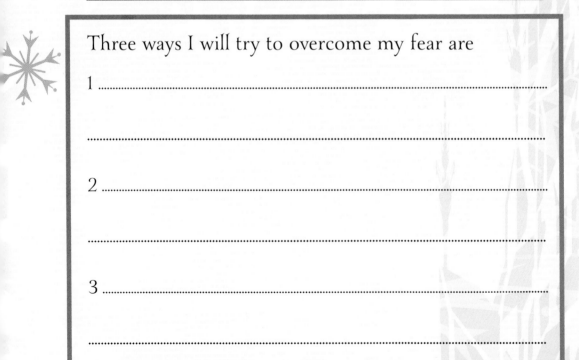

Three ways I will try to overcome my fear are

1 ....

....

2 ....

....

3 ....

....

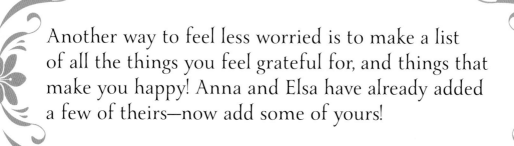

Another way to feel less worried is to make a list
of all the things you feel grateful for, and things that
make you happy! Anna and Elsa have already added
a few of theirs—now add some of yours!

The castle doors are open and I am free to explore!

My little sister and I are closer than ever.

....

....

....

....

....

Winter Wonderland

Once Elsa learns to control her icy powers, she and Anna learn to love all the magical things about winter! Snowballs, snowflakes, ice-skating, and warm winter hugs—there's so much to love about this sparkling season!

My favorite thing about winter is ....

....

My favorite winter activity is ....

....

The best way to keep warm in winter is ....

....

My favorite winter outfit is ....

....

My favorite food to eat in winter is ....

....

Every snowflake is unique—just like you!
Design your own snowflake below
using this small snowflake as a guide.

Brave and Beautiful

Anna and Elsa had to gather up all their courage to overcome their fears and save Arendelle from an eternal winter. Can you think of a time when you had to be really brave? Write about it below.

A time when I had to be really brave was

....

....

....

I find it really hard to be brave when ....

....

....

....

Use this space to write, draw, or paste in things that give you courage and make you feel brave.

Dream On, Dreamer!

When Anna was little, she used to dream of being close to her sister again. Do you have a dream for the future? Let your imagination wander and write your dream below.

My big dream for the future is ....

....

....

....

....

To make this dream come true, I need to ....

....

....

....

....

Daydreaming is a great way
to come up with new ideas!
What do you daydream about?

I often daydream about ....

....

....

My favorite place to daydream is

....

....

My craziest daydream was ....

....

....

Home Sweet Home

Anna and Elsa live in the beautiful kingdom of Arendelle. It is surrounded by crystal-clear water and majestic, snowy mountains. Anna and Elsa want to know all about your home and what makes it special to you!

I live in a place called ....

List five words below that best describe your home.

My favorite thing about my home is ....

....

Something special about my home is ....

....

My home is lots of fun because ....

....

Make a collage of pictures that remind you of your home.
Perhaps a flower that grows nearby, a food that your home
is famous for, or the color the leaves turn in fall. Be creative!

Future Friends

Anna and Elsa have made lots of new friends since opening the castle doors. Meeting new people is fun! If you could meet anyone in the world—real or imaginary—who would it be?

I would like to meet ....

A question I'd like to ask them is ....

....

Draw or paste in a picture of them here.

I would like to meet ....

....

A question I'd like to ask them is ....

....

....

....

Draw or paste in a picture of them here.

Draw or paste in a picture of them here.

I would like to meet ....

....

A question I'd like to ask them is ....

....

....

....

This or That?

Anna and Elsa's differences used to keep them apart. But now they realize it's their differences that make them special! Ask a friend to read these questions aloud to you and answer them as quickly as possible. It's time to discover and celebrate your differences!

Music or movies?

Dancing or singing?

Snowmen or sand castles?

Reading or writing?

Summer or winter?

Tiny creatures or big animals?

Roller skates or ice skates?

Action or adventure?

Cupcakes or candy?

Raindrops or snowflakes?

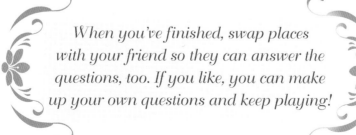

When you've finished, swap places with your friend so they can answer the questions, too. If you like, you can make up your own questions and keep playing!

List It

Anna and Elsa have so many things they want to do together, it's hard to remember them all! Use the lists below to keep track of all your amazing plans!

Places to visit

....

....

....

....

....

....

....

People to meet

....

....

....

....

....

....

....

Movies to watch

....

....

....

....

Skills to learn

....

....

....

....

Books to read

....

....

....

....

Back to Nature

Anna and Elsa love to explore the beautiful scenery and landscape of their home, Arendelle. Have you spent time exploring nature and the outdoors, or would you like to? Next time you explore outdoors, take this book with you and fill in the lines below.

I am going to explore ....
....

It could be your backyard, a garden, or a park nearby!

I can see ....

....

I can smell ....

....

I can hear ....

....

I can feel ....

....

Did you collect anything along the way? Maybe a pretty fallen leaf, a flower, or a four-leaf clover? Paste in a picture, a drawing, or the real thing here!

It's Your Day!

Anna and Elsa love to make the most of every day together. Every day is special—but some days you have to look a little harder to find the special things! Use the next few pages to help you find all the special things in each day.

Today is

Monday

Tuesday

Wednesday

Thursday

Friday

Saturday

Sunday

Draw or paste in a picture of the most interesting thing from your day.

Today I'm feeling ....

The best thing about today is ....

The worst thing about today is ....

Something new I learned today is ....

Today is special because ....

Today is

Monday

Tuesday

Wednesday

Thursday

Friday

Saturday

Sunday

Today I'm feeling ....

....

The best thing about today is ....

....

The worst thing about today is ....

....

Something new I learned today is ....

....

Today is special because ....

....

Draw or paste in a picture of the most interesting thing from your day.

Today is

Monday

Tuesday

Wednesday

Thursday

Friday

Saturday

Sunday

Today I'm feeling ....

....

The best thing about today is ....

....

The worst thing about today is ....

....

Something new I learned today is ....

....

Today is special because ....

....

Draw or paste in a picture of the most interesting thing from your day.

Today is

Monday

Tuesday

Wednesday

Thursday

Friday

Saturday

Sunday

Today I'm feeling ....

....

The best thing about today is ....

....

The worst thing about today is ....

....

Something new I learned today is ....

....

Today is special because ....

....

Draw or paste in a picture of the most interesting thing from your day.